The New Adventures of
MARY-KATE & ASHLEY ™

The Case Of The
DOG SHOW MYSTERY

Look for more great books in
~The New Adventures of~
MARY-KATE & ASHLEY™
series:

The Case Of The
DOG SHOW MYSTERY

by Melinda Metz

HarperEntertainment
An Imprint of HarperCollinsPublishers

A PARACHUTE PRESS BOOK

PARACHUTE
PRESS

Parachute Publishing, L.L.C.
156 Fifth Avenue
New York, NY 10010

 DUALSTAR
PUBLICATIONS

Dualstar Publications
1801 Century Park East
12th Floor
Los Angeles, CA 90067

HarperEntertainment

An Imprint of HarperCollins*Publishers*
10 East 53rd Street, New York, NY 10022

First printing: May 2004
Printed in the United States of America

www.mary-kateandashley.com

10 9 8 7 6 5 4 3 2 1

CLUE'S BIG MOMENT

"Clue looks beautiful, doesn't she, Mary-Kate?" my twin sister, Ashley, asked.

I studied our basset hound, Clue. We had brushed her long floppy ears twenty strokes each. We had brushed her short, stubby legs twenty strokes each. We had brushed her long, long body thirty strokes. "Absolutely beautiful," I agreed.

Ashley turned to the new friends we'd made that day, Tony and Joey LaMott. "What do you think? Is Clue ready now to

compete against all the other hounds in the State Fair Kids-with-Dogs Show?"

Tony and Joey knew everything about how dogs were judged in a show. Their dog, Bob, had already won Best of Breed in the spaniel group. That meant the judge thought Bob was the best of all the spaniels in the dog show.

Tony made three circles around Clue, saying, "Here, Clue! Look at me! Good dog!"

Joey shoved his hands into his pockets and stared at her.

Ashley and I grinned at each other. We called the brothers Tony Loud and Joey Soft. Tony talked loudly and very fast. Joey talked slowly and softly—when he talked at all. Tony was ten—a year older than Ashley and I. Joey was eight—a year younger.

"Clue looks good! She looks very, very good! I think she *will* be the winner in the hound group," Tony said. "Then she'll end

up competing against Bob for Best in Show!"

He chewed hard on a piece of strawberry gum. "Best in Show is when all the winners of each group compete against one another," Tony added.

"That would be so cool," Ashley said. "Which judge picks the dog for Best in Show?"

Tony ran his fingers though his curly brown hair. "All three judges! None of the judges is an expert on all kinds of dogs, but together they know everything."

I realized Joey was still staring at Clue. "We decided to enter Clue in the dog show because she's always working hard to help us solve our cases," I told him. "We thought this would be fun for her."

Joey didn't say anything. He didn't even blink!

"Right," Ashley agreed. "We really should call our detective agency Olsen and Olsen

and Olsen. Clue has helped us solve lots of cases with her nose. We call it her Super Sniffer. She can track down anything with her nose—anything at all."

"She's a star detective. But is she going to be a star in the dog show ring too?" I asked, trying to get Joey to speak. "What do you think, Joey?"

Joey still didn't answer. He kept staring at Clue. Ashley and I watched him watch her. In the background, water splashed in tubs and blow-dryers buzzed. Everywhere in the huge backstage area kids were grooming their pups.

"Teeth," Joey finally said.

Ashley and I stared each other. "Oh, no!" we cried together. "We forgot to brush Clue's teeth!"

"And Clue's group is onstage next!" Ashley said.

Tony looked into the ring. "Don't panic! Don't panic!" he cried. "You still have time.

They haven't finished judging the sporting dogs yet. Not even close!"

Joey quietly unzipped his backpack. He pulled out a piece of bumpy rubber and slipped it over Ashley's middle finger. "Easier than a toothbrush." He spread some doggie toothpaste on the piece of rubber. "This is how we get Bob's teeth clean."

Ashley began to scrub Clue's teeth. A speck of foam flew out of Clue's mouth and landed on her fur. "Oops. I forgot the towel." Joey slid a towel out of his backpack. He held the towel just under Clue's lower lip as Ashley brushed.

"Wow, Joey. You have a lot of dog-grooming supplies," I said. "You have that whole backpack full of stuff. And Tony has that huge purple gym bag." Tony carried that purple gym bag everywhere he went. Everywhere.

Ashley finished cleaning Clue's teeth.

"What's in there, exactly?" she asked, pointing to the purple bag.

Tony bounced up and down on his toes. "Just backups. Extra doggie shampoo, extra doggie breath spray, extra doggie fur conditioner, extra doggie toothpaste. Basically extra doggie everything."

"Yikes, Ashley. We need to go shopping at the pet store for Clue!" I told her.

"How's my favorite dog?" Eldin McBride called. He strolled over to us.

Eldin ran the backstage area of the dog show. He took care of all the dogs. He walked them in a special part of the fairgrounds for exercise. He refilled their water dishes. And he supplied the soap for bubble baths.

"Clue's great!" I answered. "It's almost her turn to go into the ring."

"Then I'll have to give her a hug when she's finished," Eldin said. He straightened his *Dog's Best Friend* baseball cap on his

head. "I don't want to mess up her fur."

He pulled a photo out of the center pocket of his overalls. "But I do want to show you this. Remember how I told you about Yancy?"

"The dog you had when you were a boy?" I asked.

"The one who looked just like Clue?" Ashley jumped in.

Eldin nodded. He turned the photo so we could see it.

"Wow!" I gasped.

"He could be your twin, Clue," Ashley told our dog.

"True," Eldin said. He knelt down so he and Clue were eye to eye. "I really miss Yancy. Clue, I wish I could take you home with me. You know that, don't you, girl?"

Clue gave him a happy tail wag.

"Mary-Kate! Ashley! It's your turn to go into the ring!" Tony cried. He waved his arms to get our attention.

"Do I look okay?" I asked Ashley softly.

She smoothed my strawberry-blond hair. Her blue eyes were bright with excitement. "Perfect," Ashley answered.

"You too," I told her. Ashley moved to Clue's left. I took my place on Clue's right. Then the three of us marched out into the ring.

Near the center of the ring sat a row of low benches. Ashley and I led Clue over to hers. "Up, girl," Ashley said. Clue hopped up onto the small bench. Ashley slipped her a little piece of hot dog.

Clue didn't seem bothered by all the people in the bleachers watching her. She stood still, head and tail up. She looked so proud of herself. But Ashley and I were twice as proud of her!

The judging began with the dog on the first bench. Everything was going just the way it was supposed to. We all looked like a picture from one of the State Fair booklets.

The people who run the State Fair sent us all kinds of information as soon as we entered Clue in the dog show. There were booklets on grooming. Booklets on training your dog. Booklets on how the dogs were judged.

Ashley and I had been getting Clue ready for the show for months. Yesterday we had a practice show in the backyard. Our little sister, Lizzie, judged it.

"The judge is almost up to Clue!" Ashley whispered.

I sneaked a peek at the judge. He was tall and bald and dressed all in black. He patted the dachshund on the bench next to Clue. Then he came toward us!

This was it. Clue's big moment!

AND THE WINNER IS . . . ?

The dog show judge ran his hands over Clue's legs. He pulled back Clue's top lip and checked her teeth. He studied the straightness of her spine.

I knew what the judge was doing. He was making sure that Clue was strong and healthy.

"Please take her out and back for me," the judge said.

Ashley took Clue's leash. "Down, girl," she called. Clue jumped off the bench.

Then Ashley and Clue trotted quickly down the row of benches and back.

Everyone in the bleachers watched Clue. So did the judge. The way a dog moves is important. I loved the way Clue's ears flopped when she ran. I thought she looked so cute!

But what did the judge think?

I took another look at him. He wasn't smiling. He wasn't frowning. Hmm.

Did the judge think Clue was as special as Ashley and I did?

Did he think she was a star?

Or not?

The judge moved on to study the next dog. I was so nervous! I felt as if I had stopped breathing until all the dogs were judged. There were two dachshunds, a fluffy tan Afghan hound, a sad-eyed bloodhound, two black-tan-and-white beagles, a skinny greyhound, a big Irish wolfhound, a basenji whose tail curled around in a knot,

and of course our own basset hound, Clue!

Now all the dogs and all the owners were waiting to hear which hound would be chosen as the *best* hound. I grabbed Ashley's hand as the judge walked to the microphone in front of the bleachers. We each put our other hand on Clue's head.

"I'm pleased to announce the Best of Breed in the hound group," the judge said. "Clue Olsen!" Everyone in the bleachers clapped and clapped.

Ashley hugged me, then hugged Clue, then hugged me again. "Clue won! She won!"

"I can't believe it!" I said, jumping up and down. "Her very first dog show!" I hugged Clue. "You're amazing!" I told her.

We hurried to the judge. He pinned a blue ribbon onto Clue's collar. I couldn't stop smiling.

The judge shook Ashley's hand, then mine. "Congratulations," he told us. "Now

go on. I think there are some people waiting to talk to you."

The judge pointed backstage. A group of reporters and photographers were waiting for us! Ashley, Clue, and I rushed over to them.

"I heard this is your first show. Is that true?" one of the reporters asked.

"How old is your dog?" another reporter asked.

"Did you work with a trainer?" a third reporter asked before Ashley and I could even answer the first question.

Then camera flashes started going off! It was as if Clue, Ashley, and I were celebrities. At least until the next part of the dog show began. Then the reporters moved back to the ring.

Joey and Tony rushed over to us. "Finally!" Tony exclaimed. "We've been trying to get to you forever!"

Joey nodded.

"Now we'll both be in the Best in Show competition! We'll get to hang out more," Tony said. "It'll be cool!"

Joey nodded again, smiling.

Ashley and I smiled back at them.

"So here's the scoop on who else is in Best in Show with us so far," Tony said. He paced back and forth in front of us. "First is a Dalmatian named Darling. Her owner is Deanna Dillinger. We've been in shows with them before."

"Doggie Deanna," Joey added.

"We call her that because dog shows are her life," Tony explained. "She doesn't do anything else. Her whole family breeds Dalmatians." He looked up. "Shh, Joey. Here she comes." Tony smiled. His smile looked kind of forced.

"Hi, Tony. Hi, Joey." Deanna walked up to us with her Dalmatian. I couldn't help giggling. Deanna looked like a Dalmatian herself. Everything she wore was white

with black polka-dots—even her sneakers— and she had a ton of freckles on her pale skin.

"This is Mary-Kate and Ashley," Joey told Deanna. "Their dog, Clue, just won in the hound group."

Deanna bent down and studied Clue more closely than the judge had. "I haven't heard of Clue. Is this your first show?"

"It is," Ashley answered. "And it's totally exciting so far."

"Well, congratulations and everything," Deanna said. "But don't get your hopes up about tomorrow, okay? Darling's won Best in Show the past three years." She ran her hand lightly over her Dalmatian's spotted head. "There's no way Clue can beat her."

"Mary-Kate, look!" Ashley said as we walked across the fairgrounds the next morning. She shook the *State Fair Dog Show Gazette* in front of my face.

"I can't see anything with you jiggling it around like that," I said.

Ashley held the newspaper perfectly still. And I saw Clue's sweet face staring back at me. I read the headline out loud. "'Clue Olsen favorite to win the Best in Show competition!'"

Ashley gave one of Clue's long, floppy ears a scratch. Clue gave a happy bark. Clue's ears are her number one favorite scratching place.

"Remember the number *three*," a girl called from behind us. We turned around. Doggie Deanna and her Dalmatian trotted over to us. Deanna held another copy of the *State Fair Dog Show Gazette* in her hand. "Three is the number of times Darling has won Best in Show."

Deanna didn't wait for us to answer. She and Darling went right to the backstage area of the dog show.

Ashley and I let her have her head start.

Then we entered the dog show's big back-stage area. A hundred smells and sounds hit us at once: dog shampoo, buzzing blow-dryers, bubble bath, kids laughing, nail polish, dogs barking. It was so exciting!

"There's my favorite dog!" Eldin cried as he rushed up to us. He carried a big purple duffel bag over one shoulder. The bag had the words DELICIOUS DOGGIE written in thread across one side.

Eldin pulled a can of what looked like hair spray out of a smaller knapsack. "This is the stuff I told you about yesterday. It will make my Clue's hair shine." He spritzed Clue from head to tail. "See?"

"Thanks, Eldin. She looks like she's been polished!" Ashley exclaimed.

"Anything for my favorite dog!" Eldin disappeared into the crowd.

"Mary-Kate! Ashley!" a familiar voice called out a second later. I looked around and spotted Tim Park, one of our very best

friends. Another one of our closest friends, Zach Jones, was with him. A little girl we didn't know was with Zach.

"We just wanted to wish you two and Clue good luck," Tim said. He took a bite of the foot-long hot dog he was holding. "Hey, I made a rhyme. You two and Clue."

"You're eating a hot dog for breakfast?" I rolled my eyes.

"It's my third," Tim answered. "I have to get my stomach stretched out for the big pie-eating contest later. I plan on winning the contest!" Tim took another big bite of his hot dog. Then he pulled yet another hot dog out of a paper bag. "Do you want one?"

"No, thanks!" Ashley said, laughing. "Do you guys want to see Clue's pen?" she asked. "All dogs have their own mini-corrals where they hang out when they aren't in the ring or with their owners."

"Yes!" the little girl cried.

"This is my cousin, Jessica," Zach said as we walked to the pen. "She loves animals. She came here yesterday with her mom." Zach was cradling the biggest watermelon I'd ever seen in his arms.

"I hope *that* isn't *your* breakfast," I said, pointing to the watermelon. "Your stomach would explode."

Zach laughed. "No way. This watermelon is going to win me a blue ribbon for the biggest homegrown melon in town. It's way too important to eat. I grew it myself in my backyard."

"Wouldn't it be cool if we all won blue ribbons at the State Fair?" Ashley asked.

"Totally cool," Zach answered. "Even Jessica is going to try to win a blue ribbon. She's competing in a tap-dance contest."

Jessica did a quick tap step. "Wish me luck," she said nervously.

"Jessica's tap show is at the same time as the Best in Show contest," Zach said.

"You'll have to tell me all about Clue's performance, okay?"

"Sure. I'm taking pictures," Ashley said.

"Here's Clue's pen," I told everyone. "And here's our friend Tony . . . in Clue's pen." I glanced at Ashley. I knew she was thinking the same thing I was—what was Tony doing in there?

"Hey," Tony said. He smiled at us. But it wasn't the kind of smile he gave us yesterday. Yesterday he gave us a big, happy smile. Today he barely managed to get the corners of his mouth up.

"What are you—" I didn't have a chance to finish asking Tony what he was doing there. Tony's brother suddenly appeared between us.

"Come on, Tony," Joey whispered.

"Gotta go," Tony called as he left Clue's pen. "We have to get Bob ready. He needs more brushing."

"Do you guys want a hot dog before you

go?" Tim asked them, reaching into his paper bag.

"We hate hot dogs," Tony answered.

Joey gave a small wave. A moment later they were gone.

"Not the friendliest guys, are they?" Zach asked.

"Joey never talks a lot. But they were both much friendlier yesterday," Ashley said.

"Sure, okay," Tim said, unconvinced. "Clue, do you want some of my hot dog?" he asked, changing the subject.

"No!" Ashley and I shouted.

"We only give her hot dogs for training treats," I explained. "We give her a piece of hot dog when she obeys a command."

"She can't have them outside the show ring," Ashley added. She took off Clue's leash and let her loose in her pen. She looped the leash over the pen's low fence.

A second later an announcement came

over the loudspeaker: "All dog owners, please come to the judging ring for new name tags. Immediately, please!"

"That's us!" I said.

We said good-bye. Then Ashley and I headed to the judging ring. There were so many kids already there, we could hardly move! But just standing in the ring was exciting. In a few hours, Clue would be in the ring too. And the judges would be deciding if she was the best dog in the whole show!

"Where do we get the name tags?" a kid shouted.

Up until now the show had been super organized. But no one seemed to know where the new name tags were. Even the judges looked confused.

"What are we doing here?" another kid asked.

"I need to go back to my dog," someone else complained.

Finally Ms. Hauser, one of the judges, made an announcement. "It seems I made a mistake. You may all return to the back-stage area."

"I want to put another coat of clear polish on Clue's nails," Ashley said.

"And we should brush her teeth again. Let's go!" I agreed.

Ashley and I raced back to Clue. We wanted to make sure she looked absolutely perfect.

"Oh, no!" I shouted when we reached the pen.

Ashley let out a cry.

The pen was empty! Clue was gone!

THE MISSING CLUE

"**C**lue has to be nearby!" I said. I tried not to panic. "The pen door is open. I bet she's just off exploring."

"Let's go find her!" Ashley said.

We rushed to the next pen. The dog—a tan pug who was a very heavy breather—sat safely inside. The pug's owner—a fourteen-year-old boy who whistled when he breathed—hadn't seen Clue.

The German shepherd with the kind brown eyes was in the next pen. His owner—

a girl with kind blue eyes—hadn't seen Clue.

The Pomeranian—a little dog with an explosion of honey-colored hair—paced around the next pen. His owner—a boy with a crew cut—hadn't seen Clue.

Darling was in her pen. Deanna hadn't seen Clue.

"Don't panic. Don't panic," I told myself. But it was getting harder to stay calm.

Bob was in his pen. Joey and Tony hadn't seen Clue.

We passed Eldin on our search. He hadn't seen Clue.

"All the other dogs are in their pens!" I burst out when we had checked them all. "Well, except Oscar. And he's not supposed to be in a pen." Oscar was the big Doberman pinscher tied up near the side entrance. He was a guard dog. The dog show used a dog as part of the show's security!

"And no one has seen Clue!" Ashley twirled a piece of her strawberry-blond

hair. She does that when she's thinking hard. "Let's go back to Clue's pen."

"Good idea," I said. "Clue probably went back there by herself."

We raced back to Clue's pen. But Clue wasn't inside. All we could do was stare at the empty space.

"Look, Mary-Kate!" Ashley grabbed my arm. "Clue's leash is missing too."

My stomach curled up into a tight little ball. "Clue couldn't have put on her leash herself," I said slowly. "That means she's not just missing. . . ."

Ashley nodded furiously. Her blue eyes were wide and serious. "That means someone stole her!"

Tears burned my eyes. "This is horrible."

"I know!" Ashley agreed. "Clue's not just our partner. She's family. We love her!"

"We have to find her!" I blinked my tears away. "And we will. We're detectives. And we have a case to solve!"

"That's right." Ashley pulled her detective notebook out of her backpack. Neither of us goes anywhere without our detective supplies. "The dog show starts after lunch. We're going to get Clue back before then."

"To get Clue back, we need clues," I said. "And the pen is the best place to start looking for them. We know that whoever stole Clue was here."

We both stepped into the pen. I checked under Clue's dog blanket. The only thing underneath was the sawdust that covered the entire floor of the pen.

Ashley lifted up Clue's water bowl. "Nothing," she muttered. She lifted up Clue's food bowl. "Nothing."

I studied each toy in Clue's toy basket. I found a lot of drool. But that was normal. Clue drools a lot.

Ashley walked around the pen, studying the floor. I checked the fence for pieces of torn cloth the dog thief might have left behind.

"I don't see anything," Ashley finally said.

"Neither do I," I answered. "But I smell—"

"—something sweet!" Ashley finished for me.

"Yes!" I agreed. "And it doesn't smell like any of the grooming stuff we used on Clue."

Ashley sniffed her arm. Then she sniffed the ends of her hair. "Or on ourselves," she added. "I mean, it doesn't smell like our shampoo or soap or anything." She began walking around the pen again.

"What are you doing?" I asked.

"I want to see if there's a place where the smell gets stronger," Ashley explained. She stopped and crouched down. "Come over here."

I rushed over. Ashley pointed to a wet spot in the sawdust in the bottom of the pen. I sniffed. "The sweet smell is definitely coming from there."

"Take a sample," Ashley said. "We need

to find out where that sweet stuff came from."

I pulled a piece of cloth out of my backpack and soaked up as much of the moisture as I could. Then I put the cloth in a plastic bag and wrote "Sample from Clue's Pen" on the front with a marker.

"Okay, we have our first clue," Ashley said. "What else do we know about our case?"

I leaned against the pen's low fence. "Hmm. Well, we know *when* Clue was stolen."

"Right. We were in the judging ring," Ashley said. "I think we were in there for about ten minutes. About 11:10 to 11:20." She wrote that down in her notebook.

"That stupid announcement!" I burst out. "We were out in the judging ring for nothing. Clue wouldn't have been stolen if we had stayed here with her!"

"That's right," Ashley said. "We got

called out to the ring for new name tags. Name tags that didn't exist. Hmm."

Ashley's "hmm" got me thinking. "Do you think the announcement wasn't a mistake, like Ms. Hauser said?" I asked. "Do you think someone made up the story about the name tags? That way they could get us away from Clue so they could steal her."

"Let's go see what we can find out," Ashley said. I followed her to the judging ring. We saw Ms. Hauser, the judge who made the announcement about the new name tags. She was sitting in the bleachers.

We hurried over to her. "Ms. Hauser, could we ask you a question please?" Ashley asked.

"It's about the name tags, isn't it?" She let out a sigh. "Everyone's been asking what the problem was. The announcement was written on a piece of paper and left on the podium by the microphone, so I read it. That's what I do with announcements."

"Who left the announcement for you?" I asked.

"It could have been anyone." Ms. Hauser took off her glasses and polished them on the front of her blouse.

"But you wouldn't read an announcement if *I* left it for you, would you?" Ashley asked.

Ms. Hauser smiled. "You caught me on that one. No, I only read announcements written on official dog show stationery."

"Do you think we could look at the announcement?" Ashley asked.

"I'm sorry. I threw it away," Ms. Hauser answered.

"Who has official dog show stationery?" I asked.

"Only people who work on the show," she told me. She looked at us closely. "You're the famous Trenchcoat Twin detectives, aren't you?" she asked.

"Um . . . yes," I said.

"I'm very curious about the announcement myself," Ms. Hauser said. She stood up. "So let's figure this out. Let's talk to the other judges."

She took us to the two other judges. And neither one knew anything about the new name tag announcement. Even the man in charge of the whole State Fair Kids-with-Dogs Show didn't know anything about the announcement.

"The four of us are the only ones who would have decided we needed new name tags," Ms. Hauser told us. "I don't know what to think. I guess the announcement will have to stay a mystery." She gave us a wave as she left us.

Ashley pushed her hair out of her face with both hands. "Okay, we know one thing for sure. The announcement was a fake."

"Right," I agreed. "All we have to do is find out who faked it—"

"—and we find Clue!" Ashley finished.

WHO COULD IT BE?

"We have a big problem," I told Ashley. "We already talked to everybody who works on the dog show. And that means we talked to everybody who has official dog show stationery."

"You're right!" Ashley frowned. "But now we know the person who stole Clue also stole some dog show stationery." She pulled out her detective notebook and a pen.

"Wait!" I grabbed her wrist before she could start to write. "I just thought of

someone else who might have stationery. Someone we didn't talk to yet. Eldin!"

"He's been so sweet to us. And to Clue. I'd hate to think he stole her," Ashley said. "But he works for the dog show. And he has a great motive—a reason to commit the crime. He said he wished he could take Clue home!"

"Because she reminds him of Yancy, the dog he had when he was little!" I agreed.

We both bolted toward Eldin's little office. It was empty. Which meant it was a perfect time for us to snoop.

"I'll look for dog show stationery in his desk," Ashley said. "You see if you can match the smell we found in Clue's pen."

"I'm on it." Eldin's whole office was packed with doggie bubble baths, doggie shampoos, doggie conditioners, and even doggie perfumes. I bet a lot of them were sweet smelling. This would take forever unless I got lucky.

I pulled the cloth out of the evidence

bag. It was still damp. I took a whiff. Then I opened the closest bottle of grooming stuff and took a sniff. It didn't match.

I moved on. I whiffed and sniffed until my nose started to itch. "We might have to trade jobs," I told Ashley when I'd tested twenty bottles.

"I can't believe I haven't found the stationery," Ashley complained. "I've been through the whole desk. Where else would someone keep paper?"

"Hi, girls!" I spun toward the voice. I felt my face turn red.

Eldin. It was Eldin. Standing in the doorway. And I was holding an open bottle of Poodle Potion in my hand!

"Eldin, hi!" Ashley said. "We were just—"

"I can see what you were doing!" Eldin said. "Getting supplies for Clue. Where is she? When did you get her back? Why didn't you bring her with you?"

"We . . . didn't find her, Eldin," Ashley

said. Her voice sounded a little shaky, and I realized Ashley was as worried about Clue as I was.

Eldin stopped smiling. "That's awful! You must miss her so much."

"We do," Ashley and I said together.

"I just hope she's okay," I admitted.

Eldin looked from Ashley to me. "I'm sure you'll find her soon," he said uncomfortably. "So . . . well, what *are* you doing in my office if you're not getting supplies for Clue?"

"We wanted to ask you about dog show stationery," Ashley said.

"I wish I'd known you two wanted some," Eldin said. "I already gave it away to the other kids."

"What other kids?" I asked.

"Well, Deanna was the first one," Eldin explained. "She came by yesterday and asked for a piece. She's making a scrapbook for Darling's Best in Show win." Eldin snorted. "I told her not to get ahead of herself. I told

her she had a lot of competition. I told her your Clue might even win."

Eldin touched the middle pocket of his overalls. That's where he kept the photo of the basset hound he had when he was a kid. I was pretty sure he was thinking about Yancy right now. He really loved that dog.

"Anyway," Eldin went on, "other kids must have heard I gave Deanna the paper. A bunch more dropped by asking for it. I would have saved you some if I knew you wanted it. But I'm all out."

"That's okay," I said. "Can you remember who else you gave it to?" I saw Ashley take out her notebook.

Eldin tugged on the bill of his baseball cap. "Tony and Joey. Nice boys. And the girl with the sweet Labrador. The boy with the dachshund. And Roger. Wait, that's the dog's name. You know who I mean?"

"Was it Anna?" Ashley suggested.

"That's the one," Eldin agreed. "And

that's about it. I didn't have many sheets to begin with. I don't really need them."

"Thanks, Eldin. We have to keep looking for Clue now," I told him.

"Let me know what happens," he called after us as we left his office.

"I think we should check out Deanna first, don't you?" Ashley asked me.

"Absolutely," I answered. "The *State Fair Dog Show Gazette* said they thought Clue was going to win."

"And Deanna is already making a scrapbook for Darling's big win," Ashley added. "She definitely has a motive."

"Yes—getting rid of the competition. Darling has a better chance to win without Clue in the show." I grabbed Ashley's hand. "Let's get over to Darling's pen and do some clue hunting."

"I'm sure Deanna will be there. I'll keep her busy. You can search," Ashley suggested.

"Great!" I cried. "We could have Clue back in a couple of minutes!"

IT'S A MATCH!

Ashley and I rushed to Darling's pen. Deanna was there. She was leaning into the pen, reading *101 Dalmatians* to Darling.

"I'll get Deanna away from the pen so you can look around," Ashley said. "I'll ask her if she wants to buy some doggie ice cream for Darling."

"Good idea!" I said. "She'll do anything for Darling."

I watched as Ashley talked to Deanna. I watched Deanna shake her head. I watched

Ashley talk some more. I watched Deanna shake her head some more. I watched Ashley talk and talk and talk.

We were doomed! There wasn't much time left to find Clue. We had to search Darling's pen. And Deanna wouldn't move.

Wait. Ashley must have come up with a new plan. She pulled out her notebook. A moment later Deanna was sitting on the floor with Ashley. They had their backs to the pen, and Deanna was drawing something in the notebook.

Ashley motioned toward the pen. It wasn't the perfect snooping situation, but it would have to do.

I hurried over to the gate leading to the pen. Then I dropped down onto my hands and knees. I figured it would be harder for Deanna to notice me down there.

I crawled inside. Darling came over to greet me. Our noses were almost at the same height. "Hi, it's me," I whispered to

her. "Don't bark, okay? I just came to hang out with you for a while."

Darling sniffed in agreement. I gave a big sniff back at her—because she smelled like a clue to me!

I pulled the evidence bag out of my backpack. Then I pulled the cloth out of the evidence bag. I sniffed the cloth. Then I sniffed Darling. I had a match! Darling smelled exactly like the sweet odor Ashley and I had noticed in Clue's pen!

"So are you counting the spots you're drawing?" I heard Ashley ask Deanna. "I mean, do all Dalmatians have exactly the same number of spots?"

Poor Ashley. She had to come up with some pretty silly questions to keep Deanna busy.

Deanna snorted. "Of course not. And sometimes the spots can be liver-colored instead of pure black."

I began to slowly crawl around the pen. The sawdust on the ground made it easy to

move silently. Darling kept me company by following me around. She was a lot friendlier than Deanna!

I spotted a large, shiny, black-and-white polka-dotted box in one corner of the pen. I decided to look in it first. I didn't know how long Ashley would be able to keep Deanna busy.

I crawled toward the box as fast as I could. I stirred up sawdust as I went. And Darling started to sneeze. Oh, no! That would definitely get Deanna's attention.

I turned around and wiped the sawdust off Darling's nose with my fingers. "Please don't sneeze," I begged her.

"If we don't find Clue, maybe we'll buy a puppy from your dad," I heard Ashley say loudly.

Ashley's voice shook when she said those words. I knew she hated to even think about never seeing our Clue again. So did I!

But it was the right thing to say. Deanna started telling Ashley all about the Dalmatians her father had for sale.

I started to crawl toward the box again. But slowly. Very, very slowly. I didn't want any sneezing.

Finally I reached the box. Darling watched as I opened the lid.

The box was full of grooming supplies. I picked up the brush lying on top and studied it. There were hairs caught in the brush—black, tan, and white hairs.

I looked at Darling. Her coat was snowy white with inky black spots. She didn't have a tan hair on her body. But I knew who did.

Clue!

A NOSE KNOWS

I jumped to my feet—and Deanna saw me! "What are you doing in Darling's pen?" she demanded.

"I'm trying to find Clue!" I shot back. "Now *I* have a question for *you*." I waved the dog brush in front of her. "Why does your brush have tan fur stuck in it?"

"*Tan* fur?" Ashley cried.

"I borrowed that brush from Eldin. Darling's brush had gotten wet," Deanna answered.

"How about if we return the brush for you?" Ashley asked.

She's brilliant. That way we could find out if Deanna was telling the truth about borrowing the brush.

Deanna shrugged. "If you want to. I'm done with it." She leaned into the pen and patted Darling. "Now would you two leave? I want to play Darling some music before the show. It calms her down."

"I have one more question," I said.

"I already told your sister everything I know about Dalmatians." Deanna sighed.

"Did you tell her why Darling smells the way she does?" I asked. "There was a sweet smell in Clue's pen after she was stolen. It smells exactly like Darling!"

Deanna's eyes narrowed into slits. "Wait a minute." She stared from Ashley to me. "Do you think *I* took Clue? That's crazy! I already have the best dog in the world!"

"Smell this." I handed the cloth from the

evidence bag to Deanna. "Why did Clue's pen smell like that if Darling wasn't in there?"

"And why would Darling be in there without *you*?" Ashley added.

Deanna's nose wrinkled. "That isn't the perfume I use on Darling," she said. "Darling, up!" Deanna patted the top of the low fence around Darling's pen. Darling immediately put her two front paws on top of it. Deanna gave her dog's head a long, long sniff.

"This is horrible!" Deanna cried. "Someone sprayed gross, cheap perfume all over Darling." Deanna entered the pen and rushed over to the polka-dot box. She pulled it open and yanked out a black-and-white polka-dot perfume bottle.

"I have Darling's perfume made just for her. She's the only dog who wears it." Deanna marched back to Ashley and me. She sprayed some of Darling's perfume into the air. It was a mix of lemon and something spicy. It wasn't sweet at all.

"Are you satisfied?" Deanna asked. "You have to leave now. The show starts in less than an hour. Darling and I have to prepare."

Ashley and I hurried away from Deanna. We only had an hour to find Clue! "Do you think Deanna took Clue?" I asked Ashley.

"Well, I want to know what Eldin says about the brush," Ashley answered. "But I don't think Deanna is the dognapper. She seemed furious that someone put that perfume on Darling."

I nodded. "So next stop—Eldin."

"Actually, let's talk to Tony first," Ashley suggested. "He's right over there. I want to ask him why he was in Clue's pen this morning."

"He has the same motive Deanna does," I agreed. "He doesn't want Clue to win the dog show. He wants his dog, Bob, to win."

We walked over to Tony. He barely smiled when he saw us.

"Did you find what you were looking for?" Ashley asked him.

"What?" Tony asked. His eyes moved back and forth. He couldn't look at Ashley or me for more than a second. "How did you—I'm not looking for anything."

"Remember this morning? You were in Clue's pen," I said. "Weren't you looking for something?"

"Oh, that. Oh, right," Tony answered. "I *was* looking for something. And I did find it. Thanks for asking." He gave us a tiny smile.

He seemed so different than he had when we first met him. What had happened to super-friendly Tony Loud? What had happened to the guy who helped Clue win first place in the hound group?

"So what was it?" Ashley asked. "What were you looking for?"

"I wasn't—" Tony began.

Joey walked up with Bob on a leash. He looked at Tony. Then he looked at us. He shook his head. "I . . . think you should tell them the truth," he said slowly.

7

TELL THE TRUTH

"**N**o!" Tony cried. He slapped his hand over his brother's mouth. "I'm not telling, and neither are you!"

"We have to know why Tony was in Clue's pen this morning!" Ashley insisted.

Joey twisted his head free of Tony's hand. "See? They think your weirdness has something to do with Clue! They probably think you stole her! Now just tell them the truth!"

That was more than Joey had ever said since we'd met him!

"No!" Tony yelled. His cheeks turned bright red.

"Okay, then *I'm* going to tell them," Joey announced. Tony tried to cover his mouth again, but Joey was ready this time. He easily slipped out of Tony's way.

"You know that big purple gym bag Tony always has with him?" Joey asked.

Ashley and I both nodded.

"Well, he lost it," Joey explained.

Tony let out a sigh of relief. "That's right. And I was looking for it in Clue's pen. Yep."

Ashley frowned. "I don't understand why you didn't just tell us that, Tony."

"Because of what's *in* the bag," Joey said. "It's his—"

Tony launched himself at his brother. He wrestled Joey to the floor. In two seconds Tony had Joey pinned to the ground.

"Okay, okay, I won't tell," Joey promised.

Then they stood up as if nothing had happened.

Joey looked at us and laughed. "They thought you were going to kill me."

"We take wrestling lessons together. We're always throwing each other to the ground," Tony explained.

"The gym bag," Joey said. Tony gave him a warning look. "It has something important in it. Something private."

"Something I really need back," Tony added. He bounced from foot to foot.

"If you tell us what it is, maybe we can help," Ashley volunteered. "We're detectives, remember?"

Tony shook his head. "Thanks, though."

"We'll keep a lookout for the gym bag anyway," I told him. I reached down to give Bob a good-bye pat. And then I smelled it again—that same sweet smell from Clue's pen.

We already knew Tony had been in the pen. The smell wasn't new evidence. But I was still really curious. "What's this smell

on Bob?" I asked. "Some kind of shampoo or perfume or what?"

Joey bent down and sniffed Bob. He wrinkled his nose.

Tony smelled Bob too. "That's strange. We don't use anything that smells like that on him. I'm surprised it doesn't make Bob gag! I wonder how he got that stuff on him."

"Me too," I told him. Then Ashley and I told the brothers good-bye, and we headed toward Eldin's office.

"It's freaky how that sweet smell keeps turning up around our suspects," Ashley commented. "Especially because they seem completely surprised to find it on their dogs."

"I know," I said. "It has to be a big clue. But I don't understand how it fits into our case at all!"

8

THE SECRET IS OUT

Ashley stopped right in the middle of taking a step. Her right foot was off the ground.

"What?" I asked her.

"Tony was looking for his purple gym bag in Clue's pen," she told me.

"I know," I answered. "Don't you want to put your foot down?"

Ashley put her foot down. "That means he must have been in Clue's pen sometime before we saw him there this morning."

"Right!" I said. Now I understood why Ashley had stopped in mid step. This was a good clue. "You don't look for something you've lost in a place you've never been before."

"Hmm. I'm thinking Tony's secret might have a lot more to do with Clue than we thought. We need to figure it out," Ashley said.

"Yep. But we have real evidence against Deanna—the tan hairs on the dog brush I found in Darling's pen," I reminded Ashley. "We should check out her story first."

"Let's run," she urged. "There's not much time left." We raced past all the kids getting their dogs ready for the Best in Show competition.

"Wait. There he is!" I yelled. I pointed to Eldin. He was gently fluffing the pom-pom on the end of a poodle's tail.

We walked over quietly. We didn't want to disturb his work or upset the dog.

"Eldin, is this one of your brushes?" I asked.

Eldin glanced at it. "It sure is," he said, taking the brush. His big purple DELICIOUS DOGGIE duffel bag sat next to him. "In fact, I brushed your Clue with that one. Any news on my favorite girl?"

"Not yet," Ashley said. "But she'll be back in time for the show!"

"Bye, Eldin," I called. Then *I* stopped with one foot in the air. I looked over my shoulder at Eldin's purple duffel bag. It was almost the same size as Tony's gym bag. And it was exactly the same color.

"What, Mary-Kate?" Ashley asked.

"You know how we said there might be a connection between Tony's secret and our case?" I asked.

Ashley nodded.

"Well, I think I know how to find out Tony's secret. Just follow my lead," I told her.

I grabbed Eldin's duffel bag and turned it so the DELICIOUS DOGGIE logo didn't show. "We need to borrow this for one minute, Eldin," I explained. "We'll be right back."

I didn't give him time to answer. I dashed off. I heard Ashley right behind me. I didn't stop running until I found Tony and Joey.

"Hey, you guys!" I shouted. I slid to a stop in front of them. "I told you we are great detectives. Look what we found." I pointed to the purple duffel bag.

"You found Tony's teddy bear!" Joey burst out.

Ashley and I stared at each other. That was the big secret? A teddy bear?

9

DOGGIE PERFUME

"You didn't have to say it so loud!" Tony told his brother. "Everyone doesn't have to know I have a . . . what you said." Tony's cheeks looked like two of the fair's prize tomatoes, they were so red.

"No one was listening," Ashley reassured him. "Everyone's too busy getting ready for the show."

Tony grabbed the handle of the purple duffel bag. The bag he thought was his. The bag I'd borrowed from Eldin.

"Um . . . Tony . . . um." All I could think to do was tell the truth. At least part of it. "I tricked you. I'm sorry. This isn't your gym bag." I turned it around so he could see the words DELICIOUS DOGGIE on the side. "It's Eldin's."

"You're mean!" Joey burst out. "Why did you do that to Tony?"

"We wanted to help him find what he lost," Ashley explained.

"And it will be a lot easier to find it now that we know what it is," I added. Which was also the truth. But not the whole truth.

"We won't tell anybody. We promise," Ashley said.

"They're detectives," Joey told Tony. He jammed his hands into his pockets. "They could help."

Tony nodded. "I don't sleep with it or anything," he muttered. "It's my good-luck bear."

I nodded back. "We've got to get this bag

back to Eldin. We'll let you know as soon as we have any news about the you-know-what."

Ashley and I hurried away. "I don't see any way a lost teddy bear could have anything to do with Clue," Ashley said with a sigh.

"Me neither. So what do we do now?" I asked.

"We could check on the other kids we know who got stationery from Eldin. If any of them have dogs who are in the Best in Show competition—" Ashley gave a long, deep sniff. "You smell like *the* smell," she announced.

"Of course I do. I have the sample in my backpack," I reminded her.

She stopped walking. I stopped too. "No. It's stronger." Ashley sniffed the top of my head. She sniffed my face. She kept on sniffing down until she reached Eldin's duffel bag. "It's coming from in there!" she cried.

I lifted the bag to my nose. Ashley was right! The sweet scent was so strong, it almost made me dizzy!

"Open it, Mary-Kate!" Ashley exclaimed.

I grabbed the zipper. Then I hesitated. "Do you think we should, Ash?" I asked. "It's not ours."

Ashley frowned. "You're right. But this could be our biggest clue to finding Clue." She put her hand over mine. "On the count of three?" she asked.

I nodded. "One, two, three!" We pulled open the zipper together.

"Wow," Ashley breathed as she peered inside the bag. "There are about a hundred bottles of Delicious Doggie perfume in here."

"And I bet I know exactly what this Delicious Doggie stuff smells like!" I exclaimed. I opened one of the bottles and squirted some perfume into the air.

"Exactly the smell we found in Clue's

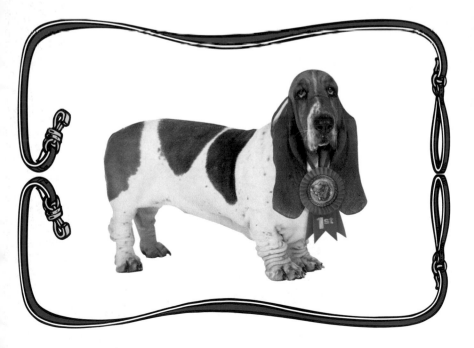

DETECTIVE TRICK

THE 1-3-5 CODE

Want to pass a secret message to your friends?
Here's a code that looks tough but is really easy
to break—if you know the trick!

1. Draw a chart like the one below, but leave the
   boxes empty.
2. From left to right, write your message in the
   boxes of the first, third, and fifth columns.
   Write only one letter in each box.
3. Fill in the remaining boxes with random letters.

Now using the 1-3-5 code, try to solve this riddle:

1	2	3	4	5
A	R	S	L	H
A	K	M	P	P
O	M	O	S	D
L	Q	E	V	!

**What dog loves to take
bubble baths?**

Write your answer below.

_____

Answer: A shampoodle!

From
The Case Of The **DOG SHOW MYSTERY**

DETECTIVE TRICK

A TOUCHY SUBJECT

**A good detective uses all of his/her senses to
solve a mystery. One of these is the sense of
touch. Try this activity and train your fingers to
do the searching.**

- Close your eyes and ask a friend to put 10 small
  items into a bag (nothing with sharp edges, please!).
- Set a timer for 2 minutes.
- Reach into the bag and feel your way around
  until the time is up.
- Take your hand out of the bag. Grab a piece of
  paper and write down all the items you touched.
- Refill the bag with different objects and have your
  friend try the same experiment.

Did you get them all?

Look for our next mystery . . .
The Case Of The **Cheerleading Tattletale**

pen," Ashley said. "And on Bob. And on Darling."

"Looks like we have some questions to ask Eldin when we return his bag," I told her. "Come on!"

We raced back to where we'd left Eldin. The poodle was gone. Eldin was gathering up his supplies.

"Eldin!" Ashley cried. "Were you in Clue's pen when Mary-Kate and I were in the judging ring this morning?"

"To get new name tags?" I added.

Eldin held up the pale green bottle he was about to put into his small knapsack. "Have I told you girls about this conditioner—Puppy Pearls?" he asked. I noticed he was speaking about three times as fast as usual. "It's the most amazing stuff. It—"

"We don't want to hear about that right now!" I burst out. "Not while Clue is missing! Please answer the question, Eldin. Were you in Clue's pen this morning?"

Eldin dropped the conditioner into his knapsack. "Yes," he admitted.

Ashley took a step closer to him. "We really need to know one more thing," she said. "Did you use your dog show stationery to ask for the name tag announcement?"

"The announcement for name tags that didn't exist? The name tags that got everyone out of the backstage area?" I said.

Eldin pulled his baseball cap low over his forehead so we couldn't see his eyes. "Yes," he confessed.

PAW PRINT PROOF

"**E**ldin! You stole Clue!" I cried.

"Where is she?" Ashley demanded. "We want her back!"

Eldin held up both hands. "No, no! You girls have it all wrong! I didn't take your Clue. I'd never do that."

"But you said you'd take her home if you could!" I reminded him.

"You said she was just like Yancy. The dog you had when you were little!" Ashley added.

"And that's why I would never, ever take her away from you. I know exactly how terrible you must feel," Eldin explained. "It's how I would have felt if someone stole Yancy."

"But you admitted you were in Clue's pen," I protested.

"And that you had Ms. Hauser make the fake announcement," Ashley added.

"That's true," Eldin said.

"I don't understand," I told him.

"I can't explain it to you," Eldin answered. He pulled his baseball cap even lower over his face. Pretty soon it would be covering his nose!

"How about if *I* explain it, Eldin," Ashley suggested.

Eldin jerked his baseball cap off his head and stared at Ashley. I was pretty surprised too. What did she know that I didn't?

"I know it wasn't only Clue's pen you went into when all the dog owners were in the judging ring," Ashley told him. "You went into Darling's pen—"

"And Bob's," I jumped in. Now I got it. Joey and Tony had told us they didn't know how the sweet smell got onto Bob. And Deanna had had a fit when she found out someone had sprayed the "cheap, gross perfume" on Darling.

"You sprayed Delicious Doggie perfume on them. And I bet you sprayed it on Clue too!" Ashley concluded.

"Yes. Okay. You're right. That's exactly what I was doing when you were in the ring!" Eldin burst out.

I shook the duffel bag full of perfume. "How many other dogs did you spray?"

Eldin squeezed his eyes closed. "All of them," he whispered. "And you know why? Because I got paid to do it! I don't even think Delicious Doggie smells that good!"

"I get it," Ashley said. "The Delicious Doggie perfume people wanted all the dogs

competing for Best in Show to wear their perfume. If the owners liked it, they might go out and buy some!"

"And they hired you to spray it on," I said to Eldin.

"They weren't sure the owners would use it if they just gave it to them," Eldin told us.

I thought about Deanna. "They were probably right," I agreed.

"I'm going to give the money back. And apologize to everyone. Right now." Eldin marched off.

"I think he's telling the truth," Ashley said.

"I don't know," I answered. "I hope he is. But he wasn't going to tell us about his deal with the perfume people, remember? He only admitted it after you figured it out."

"So you think he could be lying about Clue?" Ashley asked.

I nodded. "I think we should figure out if

he had enough time to spray all the dogs with perfume *and* steal Clue, too."

"How do we do that?" Ashley asked.

I pulled a stopwatch out of my backpack and handed it to her. "How long do you think we were in the judging ring this morning?"

"Ten minutes," Ashley told me.

"Okay, when you say *go*, I'll start running," I said. "I can't go into all the pens—the dog owners would freak. But I'll pretend to go in and spray perfume."

"If you can't do it in ten minutes, then Eldin couldn't either. You're faster than he is," Ashley said.

I nodded.

"All right. On your mark. Get set. Go!" Ashley cried.

And I was off. I stopped at the first pen. I paused to chant, "Go in, call dog, dog likes me, comes over, spray, spray, go out, close pen." I wanted to be sure to take enough time at each pen.

I raced to the next pen. I said the same words. And I took off again.

At one pen I counted to ten for a shy dog.

At another pen I counted to seventeen for a dog who really wanted to play and kept ducking away from me.

I paused at an empty pen all the way in the rear of the backstage area. Something was strange about it. But there was no time to stop.

I ran and chanted and ran until I got back to Ashley. "Time?" I asked, breathing hard.

"Ten minutes, thirty-seven seconds," Ashley announced. "That means Eldin was probably telling the truth. He didn't have time to spray all the dogs *and* steal Clue."

"But what if he didn't spray *all* the dogs?" I asked. He could have sprayed some of the dogs but not every last one. Running around to every pen hadn't proved anything after all.

Ashley nibbled her lower lip. "We have less than half an hour until the show starts! And no new clues."

Then something occurred to me. "I think I know where to get some! Come on!" I took Ashley by the wrist. I tugged her over to the empty pen in the back.

"There's no water or food in here. Not even any sawdust," Ashley observed. "No one's been using this pen."

"That's why I thought it was weird that there were paw prints in it!" I exclaimed. "Do you have Clue's dog show application with you? I want to compare her 'pawto-graph' to the prints."

Ashley had the application out of her backpack in a flash. We both studied the prints in the dirt and the ink print of Clue's paw at the top of the application.

"It's hard to tell . . ." I began. "But it looks like a match!"

DANGEROUS DOBERMAN

We hurried into the pen and carefully followed the prints. We wanted to trace every single step Clue had taken.

"She sat in this spot," Ashley said.

"Oh, Ash! I bet she was trying to see us! Her real pen is in that direction," I cried and pointed.

We continued following Clue's prints. "She snooped behind these boxes," Ashley commented.

We pushed the cardboard boxes aside—

and found Tony's purple gym bag! I unzipped it.

"Huh. No teddy bear," Ashley said.

"But there is a big glob of drool!" I said.

Ashley and I grinned at each other. Spaniels—like Joey and Tony's dog—don't drool a lot. Bob wouldn't have gotten the glob of drool into the gym bag.

But basset hounds like Clue—they live to drool!

"Hey, Ashley, look!" I pointed to some cardboard hot-dog containers and some half-eaten hot dogs.

"It's weird that those are back here with Tony's gym bag," Ashley said. "Tony said he and Joey both hate hot dogs."

"I know." I put the hot dogs and containers into evidence bags. "This case keeps getting stranger and—"

"Will the dogs and owners for Best in Show please line up," a voice over the intercom said.

There was a flood of sound as dogs' names were called all over the backstage area. Leashes were snapped on and pen doors opened.

"Clue is going to miss her chance if we don't hurry," I said.

"I know! I know!" Ashley answered. "But we're close to finding her. I know it."

I rushed out of the pen and stood on tiptoe. "I can see Deanna and Darling lining up. And Joey and Bob. I don't see Tony though."

"I do!" Ashley cried. "He just went running out the side door! And I want to know why!"

"Me too!" We raced toward the side door.

"Stop, Mary-Kate! Look out!" Ashley shouted.

I didn't need her warning. I'd already seen him—Oscar, the security dog.

The huge Doberman pinscher was loose.

He blocked our way to the door. And he did not look happy.

"Maybe we should just back up a step," I whispered. I took a step backward.

Oscar crouched down low. He looked ready to pounce. Then he pulled back his lips in a snarl.

I'd never seen so many teeth!

12

NICK OF TIME

"**O**kay, we can't back up," I whispered. "Oscar doesn't like it."

"And we can't run forward," Ashley whispered.

Oscar growled. His white teeth glistened.

My heart beat triple time.

I got an idea. I was still holding the evidence bag. And in the evidence bag was . . . a hot dog.

"Get ready to go," I told Ashley. I tore

open the bag and hurled the hot dog as far as I could. "Hot dog, Oscar! Go, go, go!" I yelled—half to Oscar, half to Ashley.

Ashley and I ran. So did Oscar. But Oscar ran toward the hot dog. We ran out the door.

"I see Tony!" Ashley exclaimed as we left the building. "He's over there by the jam display."

We put on speed as we zoomed past the rows of homemade jams. We zigzagged though the game arcade and around the super slide. We lost Tony at the yodeling contest, but I spotted him a few seconds later heading toward the Tip-Top Tap recital.

Ashley and I ran even harder. I could almost grab Tony by the back of the shirt.

"Tony, just stop!" Ashley yelled. "We have to talk to you!"

Tony dove into the crowd of people watching the tap dancers. "Excuse us.

Excuse us," Ashley said as we pushed our way after him.

"We're going to get him!" I said. "He's going to bump into the stage in a second, and we'll get him!"

But Tony didn't stop at the edge of the stage. He slid right under it!

"What is he doing?" I shouted.

"Let's find out!" Ashley shouted back. She dove under the stage after Tony. I dove after her.

I could hear the *clomp-clomp* of tap dancers on the wooden stage above my head. It sounded as if they were going to break through the wooden planks and come down on top of us.

I crawled as fast as I could though the darkness. Dirt coated my hands and filled my nose.

A second later I saw light. Ashley grabbed my hand and pulled me out from under the stage. It was like stepping into a

field of sunflowers. The next group of little girl tap dancers about to perform was gathered backstage. They all had on bright yellow flower costumes.

Tony stood in the center of the cluster of little girls. Jessica, our friend Zach's cousin, stood next to him, holding a giant teddy bear. And on Tony's other side sat . . . Clue!

"Good girl," Tony muttered. He slipped Clue a piece of hot dog.

Tony stared at us for a long moment. Then he smiled. "I found your dog," he said.

I put my hands on my hips. "You mean you *stole* our dog," I corrected him. "We found hot dogs in the empty pen where she left her paw prints. You gave Clue hot dogs to get her to come with you."

"Because you wanted to use Clue's Super Sniffer to find your teddy bear!" Ashley added.

"Right," I jumped in. "That's why we found the glob of drool in your duffel bag.

You had her smell the bag to get the teddy bear's scent. But where did you find the bag?"

"I found it in a pen that wasn't being used. But the bag was empty," Tony said. "So I took Clue to the empty pen. I thought if she could smell the bag, it would help her sniff out the teddy bear for me."

"So you admit that you stole her!" I said.

"Why didn't you just ask to borrow Clue?" Ashley asked.

"I couldn't ask you to help me find a *teddy bear*!" Tony exclaimed. He shook his head. "I know I shouldn't have taken Clue. But I was going to bring her back before the last competition."

"But you didn't!" I said. "It's already starting."

"I know. I *was* bringing Clue back," Tony told Ashley and me. "Then she went crazy. She got away from me. When you were chasing me, I was chasing her!"

"Jessica, did you walk by the dog show a little while ago?" I asked.

Jessica nodded.

"That's why Clue took off on you," Ashley explained to Tony. "Her Super Sniffer got the teddy bear's scent."

I reached out and patted the teddy bear Jessica held in her arms. "Where did you get this?" I asked her.

"You know where she got it! She stole it from me!" Tony shouted.

"And you stole Clue from us," Ashley reminded him.

"I went to see the dogs with Zach," Jessica said. Then she pointed at Tony. "I overheard him say the teddy bear was lucky. And I needed luck for the recital. I was going to bring it back."

Jessica held the teddy bear out to Tony. "I'm sorry I took your bear."

"Keep it till after the show," Tony told her. He turned to Ashley and me. "I'm really

sorry I took your dog. You guys should take Clue and go back to the show. You can probably still make it," he said. "They have you line up a long time before you actually start."

"Let's go!" Ashley said.

Clue couldn't run too fast—not with all the hot dogs bouncing around in her stomach. But we made it back just in time to march out into the ring with the others.

I didn't know how the judges made their decisions. How do you choose between the spaniel, Bob, and a Yorkshire terrier? Or a beautiful red Irish setter and polka-dotted Darling? Or a Chihuahua and Clue?

But the three judges decided that the Chihuahua was the best dog in the whole show. Darling came in second. And Bob came in third.

And Clue got the coolest prize—Rookie of the Year.

"You did great in your first dog show,"

Ashley told Clue as Ms. Hauser pinned the silver Rookie ribbon onto Clue's collar.

I gave Clue a hug. "We're so glad we got you back!"

"Yeah, we love you!" Ashley gave Clue a hug, too.

Clue gave a *woof*! She wagged her tail hard. It was her way of saying she loved Ashley and me too.

"You may not be the Best in Show," I told Clue, "but you're the best dog in the whole wide world to us!"

Hi from both of us,

Ashley and I couldn't wait for the Cheerlympics to start. Ashley is the captain of our cheerleading squad here at Camp Pom-Pom, and she wrote all our cheers herself.

But on the very first day, the Pirates squad stole our cheer—and our great dance moves too! We had to find out who was spying on us before we lost the entire Cheerlympics! Want to find out what happened? Check out the next page for a sneak peek at *The New Adventures of Mary-Kate & Ashley: The Case of the Cheerleading Tattletale.*

See you next time!

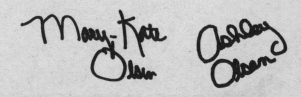

A sneak peek at our next mystery…

The Case Of The

Cheerleading Tattletale

"Welcome to Camp Pom-Pom!" Ms. Braun said to the crowd. "It's time for the second contest in the Cheerlympics—the Spirit Cheer."

I stood at the edge of the field with the rest of my squad, the Eagles.

Ashley had made up our Spirit Cheer— the words, the moves, everything. Instead of carrying pom-poms, we were wearing drums around our necks. That was Ashley's idea, too. She wanted to beat the drums as we marched out onto the field. The drums would make our cheer a winner for sure!

"And here come the Pirates!" Ms. Braun announced.

The Pirates were the team we had to beat to win the contest.

Boom! Boom! Boom!

The Pirates marched onto the field.

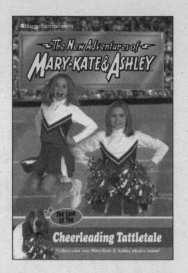

Boom! Boom! Boom!

My mouth dropped open. So did Ashley's.

"They're all wearing drums!" I cried.

The Pirates started their cheer.

Can you hear the beat? Start clapping!

Can you feel the beat? Start stamping!

"Those are the words to *our* Spirit Cheer!" I said to Ashley. "No way is this a coincidence!"

"You're right," Ashley said. She looked really worried. "They stole our cheer—again!"

TWO of a kind™
BOOK SERIES

Based on the hit television series

#35 TWO of a kind Diaries

mary-kate olsen ashley olsen

Camp Rock 'n' Roll

Mary-Kate and Ashley are off to White Oak Academy, an all-girl boarding school in New Hampshire! With new roommates, fun classes, and a boys' school just down the road, there's excitement around every corner!

Coming soon wherever books are sold!

Don't miss the other books in the TWO of a kind™ book series!

- ❏ It's a Twin Thing
- ❏ How to Flunk Your First Date
- ❏ The Sleepover Secret
- ❏ One Twin Too Many
- ❏ To Snoop or Not to Snoop?
- ❏ My Sister the Supermodel
- ❏ Two's a Crowd
- ❏ Let's Party!
- ❏ Calling All Boys
- ❏ Winner Take All
- ❏ P.S. Wish You Were Here
- ❏ The Cool Club

- ❏ War of the Wardrobes
- ❏ Bye-Bye Boyfriend
- ❏ It's Snow Problem
- ❏ Likes Me, Likes Me Not
- ❏ Shore Thing
- ❏ Two for the Road
- ❏ Surprise, Surprise!
- ❏ Sealed with a Kiss
- ❏ Now You See Him, Now You Don't
- ❏ April Fools' Rules!
- ❏ Island Girls
- ❏ Surf, Sand, and Secrets

- ❏ Closer Than Ever
- ❏ The Perfect Gift
- ❏ The Facts About Flirting
- ❏ The Dream Date Debate
- ❏ Love-Set-Match
- ❏ Making a Splash!
- ❏ Dare to Scare
- ❏ Santa Girls
- ❏ Heart to Heart
- ❏ Prom Princess

Books for Real Girls™

mary-kateandashley™
fragrances

jasmine spice

juicy peach freesia

Real Scents for the Real Girls.

www.mary-kateandashley.com

mary-kateandashley
Year of Celebration! Fashion Dolls

"We're the Class of 2004! Our senior year is going to be a blast!"

"Look for our fashion dolls celebrating our birthday and join in the fun!"

Graduation Celebration
"From prom to graduation, this will be the best year of our lives!"

Senior year stylish fashions.

Real Dolls for Real Girls.

mary-kate olsen   ashley olsen   eugene levy

new york minute

IN THEATERS MAY 7th